ISBN 0-312-01041-9

First Edition

10 9 8 7 6 5 4 3 2 1

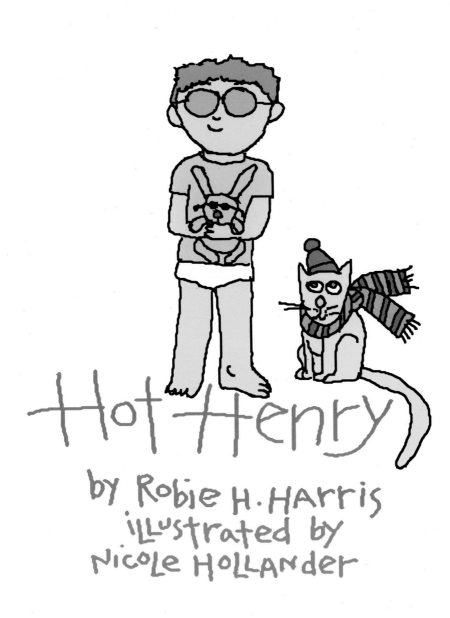

Hot Henry

by Robie H. Harris
illustrated by
Nicole Hollander

St. Martin's Press
New York

It's tir
to get
dressec

Henry watched the snow whirl and swirl in the wind.
"It's time to get dressed," said his mother.
"I don't want to get dressed," said Henry.

Henry ran to the front hall mirror.
"I like me . . . just like this!" he shouted.
"You can't go to the party in underpants," said his father.
"It's too cold."

Henry wiggled and squiggled as his mother dressed him.
He squirmed when his father tied a scarf around
his neck.
He screeched when his mother pulled his hood up and
tied it tight.

Henry ran to the window.

"It's cold out . . ." he said. "But Henry's hot.

"Henry's too hot!" he said in a very loud voice.

Henry took off his mittens and dropped them on the floor.

He untied his scarf, yanked off his hood, and pulled off his jacket.

He took off his snow boots and his snow pants, his socks
and his corduroy pants, his sweatshirt and his T-shirt,
and dropped everything
in one big pile
on the floor.

The only thing left on Henry was his underpants.

Henry's mother and father came in the living room.
"Oh, Henry! What have you done?" she asked.
"We'd better get you dressed again," said Henry's father.
"No!" yelled Henry. "Don't dress me! I can do it . . .
  all by myself!"

Henry grabbed his T-shirt and put his legs through
the arms.

He put his legs through the arms of the sweatshirt too.

He wound the scarf around and around his chest.
He wrapped the legs of his snow pants around his neck.

His jacket went on upside-down and backward.
Henry asked his father to zip up his jacket and he did.

Henry put a mitten on each foot and a sock on
each hand.

He did put his snow boots on his feet.

And then, he put a wool hat . . . on his head.

"Are we going to let him go—dressed like that?" asked
  Henry's father.

"I don't think we can dress him again," said Henry's
  mother.

"Then let's go," said Henry's father.

"Wait!" yelled Henry. "I'm not all dressed!"
He ran to his room.
He grabbed his sunglasses and put them on.

He ran to the front hall mirror and looked at himself.
He smiled.
"I like me like this!" said Henry. "Let's go!"

Henry's father opened the front door. The snow was
whirling and swirling.

"It's cold," said his mother.

"It's very cold," said his father.

"It's not cold and I'm not cold!" shouted Henry. "I'm hot!
I'm hot Henry!"

Hot Henry